The Ice-Cream Machine

Julie Bertagna

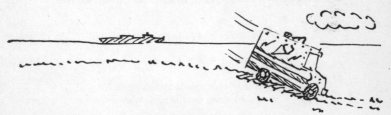

Illustrated by
Guy Parker-Rees

mammoth

To Mum, who makes the best ginger ice-cream

J.B.

For Aiko

G.P–R.

First published in Great Britain in 1998
by Mammoth, an imprint of Egmont Children's Books Limited
Michelin House, 81 Fulham Road, London SW3 6RB

Text copyright © 1998 Julie Bertagna
Illustrations copyright © 1998 Guy Parker-Rees

The rights of Julie Bertagna and Guy Parker-Rees to be identified as
the author and illustrator of this work have been asserted by them
in accordance with the Copyright, Designs and Patents Act 1988

ISBN 0 7497 3418 3

10 9 8 7 6 5 4 3 2 1

A CIP catalogue record for this book
is available from the British Library

Printed in Great Britain by Cox & Wyman Ltd,
Reading, Berkshire

Contents

~

1 Fizzbomb ice-cream

'Oh, help,' wailed Wendy Potts, and she dropped her schoolbag in horror.

Her brother Wayne groaned. 'Looks like our crackpot parents have had another one of their potty ideas,' he declared.

The two children stared in dismay at a large, lopsided vehicle which sat in the driveway of their house. Mum was sloshing soapsuds all over it. Gradually, as she hosed

off the soap, a very strange-looking van emerged. Chipped and faded stars and ribbon stripes were painted all over its bashed body. Coloured light bulbs framed its serving window. A large loudspeaker horn sat on its roof.

'It's an ice-cream van!' gasped Wayne.

'Wow!' exclaimed Wendy.

'An ice-cream van might be more fun than a herd of goats,' considered Wayne. 'Mum and Dad weren't much use as goat farmers. And an ice-cream van won't munch up the back garden.'

'It won't make the entire house smell of stinky socks either,' said Wendy. 'Remember when Dad turned the kitchen into a goats' cheese factory? Pooh!'

Wendy and Wayne held their noses at the awful memory.

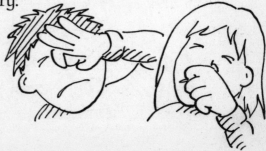

'Hello, my little Potts,' Mum called over. 'Well, what do you think of our new idea? It's our best yet – Potts of Ice-cream is going to make us pots of money!'

'Hmmm,' said Wayne.

'It's a bit tatty,' said Wendy. 'If you ask me,' she muttered as she looked at the van's peeling paint, scratched bodywork and bashed front bumper, 'you belong in a scrapyard.'

The bumper promptly clanged to the ground, just missing Wendy's foot.

'You'll never guess where I found her,' said Mum, patting the van proudly. 'Sitting right at the back of Buddy's Scrapyard. She needs a bit of attention, of course, but we'll have her ship-shape in no time, won't we?'

'Think I've got homework,' Wendy said quickly, and escaped into the house before Mum could hand her a polishing cloth.

'Me too,' said Wayne, and he ran in after his sister.

Both children were fed up helping out with Mum and Dad's madcap ideas, only to see each and every one end in disaster almost before it had begun.

In the kitchen, Dad was spooning great dollops of ice-cream into tubs.

'Taste this,' he said. 'And this. Oh, and some of this.'

'Mmm, strawberry,' said Wendy. 'Ooh, it's stingy!'

'Strawberry with a hint of hot chilli pepper,' said Dad. 'Stingy Strawberry? Now, that's just the name for it!'

'This one's all squidgy and chewy and yummy,' said Wayne.

'Marshmallow Squidge,' said Dad, scribbling

down the name. 'Excellent. Now, here's Turkish Delight with chocolate sauce.'

'It wobbles,' laughed Wayne, licking runny chocolate sauce from the jellyish ice-cream. 'Chocwobble!'

'Garden peas with mint sauce and cheese crackles.' Dad held out the spoon to Wendy.

'Cheesy Peasmint,' she giggled.

Wayne licked another spoon. 'Hmm. Cream of tomato soup.'

'With extra-tangy sauce,' said Dad, squirting bright red tomato sauce on top. 'Isn't this the most exciting ice-cream you've ever tasted?'

Wendy and Wayne nodded. It was certainly the strangest.

'Mum, have you seen Gina?' asked Wendy. 'Her supper's ready.'

'That pest of a goat has been under my feet all day,' complained Mum. 'She *will* sleep in the most inconvenient places. We should have packed her off to the farm with the rest of the herd.'

'We would have if she hadn't been snuggled under a pile of washing when we were rounding up the other goats,' Wayne remembered.

'And when I found her she gave me such a gooey look I let her stay,' chuckled Mum. 'So it's my own fault. Have you looked for her in the ice-cream van? She seems to have taken a liking to it.'

Wendy opened the back door of the ice-cream van. There was an odd rainbow glow inside. The sweet mustiness of an old chocolate box mingled with a waft of salty sea smell. Mum had swept out sand and seashells from the corners and shelves. 'It must have been a seaside ice-cream van,' she said.

There was also a strong smell of goat. And the sound of snoring.

Gina the goat lay fast asleep under the

serving counter. A sliver of something soggy hung from her lips.

'You've been guzzling newspapers again, haven't you, silly?' scolded Wendy. 'I just hope they're not today's.'

The goat started awake guiltily. She looked at Wendy with eyes as soft as fudge.

'It's no good looking at me as if newspaper wouldn't melt in your mouth,' said Wendy. 'Now come on, there's scrambled egg for you in the kitchen.'

Wendy shovelled Gina out of the van with her foot. Then she stood for a moment to look around.

On the serving counter sat a large, old-fashioned metal till with peacocks engraved all over its sides. When Wendy pressed a button, the till pinged open and all the eyes in the metal peacock tails winked.

With her sleeve, she rubbed dust from the wooden counter and it gleamed like a polished chestnut. When she looked up she saw that mottled glass tiles covered the ceiling, and it was these that made the shimmery rainbow glow. With shelves of shiny sweets and a freezer full of Dad's exciting ice-creams, it would be an Aladdin's cave of goodies!

Wendy was just about to go when she noticed something on one of the shelves. She took down the faded yellow packet.

Fizzbomb Sherbet, she read in patchy, glittery lettering.

A long, hungry baa came from outside the van. Wendy stuffed the packet of sherbet in her pocket and hurried out to Gina, who was headbutting the side of the van. A sudden angry jangle of music blared from the loudspeaker horn on the roof and Gina jumped back in fright.

'That'll teach you,' giggled Wendy.

In the kitchen, Wayne was guzzling the Marshmallow Squidge he was supposed to be stirring before it was put in tubs in the freezer.

'Look what I found.'

Wendy put the packet of Fizzbomb Sherbet in front of his marshmallowed face. 'It was in the – ow, Gina! Give it back, you greedy goat.'

But Gina had clamped her teeth tight upon the sherbet packet and was tossing her head this way and that to yank it out of Wendy's grip.

'Wayne, help!' cried Wendy.

Wayne tried tickling the goat. He tried prising her mouth open with a wooden spoon. He even tried sitting on her back and jumping up and down as if he were a cowboy on a wild horse.

But Gina only got more and more frantic, until the packet of Fizzbomb Sherbet ripped open and glittery orange powder scattered all over the kitchen.

'She's eating the sherbet packet,' yelled Wendy.

'It's everywhere,' groaned Wayne. 'A whole lot of it landed in the Marshmallow Squidge. Dad'll go mad.'

Pip-pip-POP-zip-zap-ZOP!

'What was that?' said Wayne.

'Look!' said Wendy.

The bucket full of Marshmallow Squidge was popping and fizzling so violently it was hopping across the floor. And Gina had begun to buck around the kitchen, making hiccupy baaing noises, her eyes wide with fright.

The goat opened her mouth. 'Baa-aa-zap-zip-zop-pop-pip-pip-POP!'

'She's making the same noise as the bucket,' said Wayne. 'And look at her tummy.'

Poor Gina's tummy was shuddering and juddering as if she had eaten a plateful of jumping beans. She looked at Wendy and Wayne mournfully and her eyes watered until they looked like hot fudge sauce.

'The Fizzbomb Sherbet!' Wendy and Wayne exclaimed. 'It must be that.'

'What's all the commotion?' said Dad as he came in carrying another bucketful of ice-cream mixture. 'Gina!'

He dragged the goat out from under the table where she was cowering, cross-eyed and trembling. Although the worst of the sherbet explosions had calmed, she still hiccuped the occasional pip-pop.

'Dad –' Wendy began.

'Not now, Wendy, I'm too busy. I want you all out, the lot of you. Go and pester – I mean, help – your mother until bedtime.'

'We'd better tell Mum,' Wayne whispered to his sister as they went out to the ice-cream van. 'That sherbet has done something very odd to the Marshmallow Squidge. And Gina.'

Mum put down her polish and looked at Gina who was still twitching and rolling her eyes.

'Has that goat been eating something she shouldn't again?' she demanded. 'If she's made herself sick on

ice-cream she's getting packed off to the farm tomorrow.'

Wendy and Wayne looked at each other. Gina was a pest but they had grown fond of her.

'We'll sort things later,' Wendy whispered to Wayne, as they dragged Gina into the back garden where she couldn't get into mischief. 'When Mum and Dad are asleep.'

In the middle of the night, when the house was quiet, Wayne and Wendy crept downstairs to the kitchen.

'I hope he's labelled them,' said Wayne, opening the freezer to find the shelves jam-packed with ice-cream tubs.

'There it is,' said Wendy. 'Marshmallow Squidge. And here's another, and another. Oh no, there are *loads* of them.'

'Well, we'll have to taste them all just to check if they're OK,' said Wayne firmly. 'After all, Gina's fine now.'

He looked at the goat who was fast asleep on the kitchen floor and put an ear to her tummy.

'Not a pop to be heard.'

'And it's only sherbet,' said Wendy, taking up a spoonful of Marshmallow Squidge. 'Oh, this is really yumtious.'

The ice-cream slipped down, cold and sweet. It fizzled gently as it slid to their stomachs. The fizzling grew stronger and louder until Wendy and Wayne felt most peculiar. It grew to such a pitch they felt as if they had swallowed firecrackers. In a moment they were so full of fizzbomb explosions they worried that they might launch into space like small rockets.

'Pip-pip-POP-zap-zip-ZOP!' said Wendy and Wayne when they opened their mouths for another spoonful. For, strange though it was, the fizzbomb ice-cream was the most delicious they had ever tasted. It tingled like the fizziest lemonade, was as smooth and melting as the finest chocolate, and as mouth-fillingly satisfying as the best apple crumble.

'Woosh!' said Wayne, and he reached for yet another spoonful.

Wendy put the lid firmly back on the tub.

'But, Wendy, there are tubs and tubs of Marshmallow Squidge. Shouldn't we test them all?' Wayne said hopefully.

'Better not,' said Wendy. 'Too much might blow your head off.'

'Wayne! Wendy!' Mum stood yawning in the doorway. She glared at the two of them. 'That ice-cream is not for you to guzzle. Back to bed at once.'

'I think we should tell her,' mumbled Wendy.

'Tell me what?' demanded Mum. 'What have the pair of you been up to?'

'Mum, there's something funny about that Marshmallow Squidge. You see, Gina –'

'That goat again! No, don't tell me any more, Wayne. Tomorrow is our first ice-cream run and I need sleep, not nightmares about Gina ruining things. If I had the time I'd pack her off to the farm first thing. I want Potts of Ice-cream to be a success.'

'It's nothing to worry about,' said Wayne hurriedly.

'We'll see that Gina behaves,' promised Wendy.

'This will either be the biggest disaster Mum and Dad have ever had, or it just might be an ice-cream sensation,' yawned Wendy, as she climbed into her top bunk. 'That ice-cream is very strange but it's so yummy.'

'Mmm,' said Wayne, licking bits of Marshmallow Squidge from his fingers.

'Maybe Mum and Dad have finally hit on something.'

'With a little help from Gina and the Fizzbomb Sherbet!' giggled Wendy. 'If only they knew.'

Outside, in the glow of the streetlamp, the ice-cream van gleamed from all Mum's painting and polishing.

Wayne opened the window to look.

'Night, ice-cream van,' he called. 'Tell me, are you hiding any more of that Fizzbomb Sherbet?'

An odd-sounding jangle of music suddenly

burst from the van's loudspeaker horn. One of its headlamps flashed.

'Ice-cream vans don't usually laugh, do they?' said Wayne.

'They don't usually wink either,' said Wendy. 'But I think that one just did.'

2 Macaroni comes to town

'Some greedy goat – or greedy guts – has scoffed so much Marshmallow Squidge they deserve to be sick,' announced Dad, piling tubs of ice-cream into the van's freezer.

Wendy and Wayne avoided his eye.

Mum was knee-deep in sweets and crisps. The ice-cream van's shelves were crammed full of bright and shiny wrappers that reflected in the mirror tiles and turned the back of the van into a magical cave, brimming with rainbow dazzle.

'Wow!' gasped Wayne.

'That's the ice-cream done,' said Dad.

'So we're all set,' grinned Mum.

'Though we'll be lucky if this old wreck

gets going,' muttered Dad.

'Of course she will!' cried Mum.

The van gave a judder and a toot, and an indignant jangle of music burst from its loudspeaker horn.

'She did it again!' whispered Wendy, as they all spilled out to have a look at the van.

It still had a bashed and lopsided look. But every bit of the ice-cream van, even the dented front bumper, gleamed. All its stars and ribbon stripes were now painted in vivid reds and blues and yellows.

Dad hugged Mum.

'She's a beauty. A rugged one, but a beauty all the same.'

The ice-cream van gave a happy jangle of music and flickered its coloured lights.

'You know, I'd swear that van had a mind of her own,' said Mum. 'Give me a leg up, Sam. One last thing to fix.'

Mum clambered on to the bonnet with a screwdriver. Balancing on her toes, she fiddled about with the loudspeaker horn on the roof. She fished about inside, then reached in and pulled. She pulled and pulled some more, until at last something shot out of the loudspeaker horn.

The red and blue object whacked off Dad's head then landed beside Gina who was snoozing on the lawn. She opened one eye and dreamily began to chew it.

'It's a beach-ball. A burst beach-ball,' said Wayne examining it.

'And there was all that sand and those shells inside,' Mum remembered. 'I knew this van was from the seaside.'

'A beach-ball!' Dad shook his head in bemusement. 'Well, that beats everything.'

At exactly six o'clock, the Potts family took their seats in the ice-cream van.

Dad turned the key in the ignition. The van juddered and shuddered.

'First night nerves,' said Mum. She patted the dashboard soothingly.

The van gave one last great tremble, hiccuped a burst of music, and they were off!

'The music sounds all wrong,' commented Wayne after a while. 'It's not really a tune at all.'

'It sounds back to front,' said Wendy, listening closely.

'That's it,' said Wayne. 'Silly van.'

The music hiccuped to a halt.

'Now you've done it,' said Dad. 'She's taken a huff.'

There was the yowling sound of music rewinding at top speed, another hiccup, then the tune of 'Yankee Doodle Dandy' played out strong and clear from the loud-speaker horn.

The four Potts sang along at the tops of their voices:

> *'Yankee Doodle came to town*
> *Riding on a pony,*
> *Stuck a feather in his cap*
> *And called it*
> *MACARONI!'*

'I've been wondering what we should call her,' said Mum. 'That'll do. I hereby name this ice-cream van Macaroni.'

At the swing park, Dad pulled to a stop. Almost right away a small crowd gathered round the van.

'Look, our very first queue,' sighed Mum. 'Ow, Gina! How did you sneak in? Now, what can I get you?'

Mum stepped over Gina and turned with a smile to her first customer, a dark-haired boy who was frowning up at the menu of ice-creams that Wayne and Wendy had written out and stuck to the serving window.

'I'd just like an ordinary ice-cream,' he said.

'We don't do ordinary ice-cream,' Mum said proudly. 'Why not try some Carrot and Coconut Cooldown? Or some Chocwobble?'

'Or Marshmallow Squidge,' Wayne giggled to Wendy. 'A really extraordinary ice-cream.'

'Good idea, Wayne,' said Mum. 'In fact, I'll give you a free trial,' she said to the boy. 'You are our very first customer.'

'Let's get out,' whispered Wendy. 'I want to see this.'

'Mmm,' the boy was nodding to his friends. 'This one's pretty good. In fact,' he took a great slurp, 'it's pretty galumptious-ip-pip-POP!'

The boy snapped his mouth shut as the sherbet began popping.

'Fizzbombs away!' giggled Wayne.

The dark-haired boy opened his mouth a crack. 'HEL-POP!' he yelled. 'Help-ip-pip-zip-zop-ZAP!'

'What's up, Hugo?' somebody asked.

'Zip-zap!' he said through gritted teeth. Then, after a moment, he opened his mouth and took another lick of the Marshmallow Squidge. He grinned at the crowd which had gathered round him. 'This stuff's totally amaz-zap-zap-zip-pip-pip-POP!'

25

The crowd surged back round the ice-cream van. Everyone wanted to try the strange Marshmallow Squidge ice-cream.

'An ice-cream sensation,' said Dad proudly, as they drove away from the swing park, where the racket of fizzbomb explosions was now at an eardrum-popping level. 'We're completely sold out of Marshmallow Squidge, though we might have a tub or two at home. But I don't understand all that zapping and popping. It didn't do that when I tasted it.'

'Mmm. Wonderful,' said Mum tasting the last dregs from the ice-cream scoop. 'Sam,

I hope you can remember the recip-pip-pip-POP!'

Wendy and Wayne looked at each other.

'Um, Da-ad,' said Wayne, 'we tried to tell you before. You see, there was this packet of Fizzbomb Sherbet that Wendy found in the van . . .'

'Gina got hold of it and started munching and it scattered everywhere, all over the kitchen,' continued Wendy.

Wayne and Wendy told how some Fizzbomb Sherbet had landed in a bucketful of Marshmallow Squidge and how both the ice-cream and the goat began popping and zapping.

'And now there isn't any more Fizzbomb Sherbet,' finished Wendy.

'Knew it was too good to be true,' Dad sighed. 'Never mind.'

'JANGLE!' said Macaroni.

'Sometimes,' said Mum, 'you'd think that van was trying to talk.'

'But she is!' said Wendy. 'I know she is.'

'There *is* something special about this van,' agreed Wayne. 'She winks too, and I'm sure I once heard her laugh.'

'That's because she's a magical ice-cream van,' said Wendy. 'She's full of magic – like the Fizzbomb Sherbet.'

'If this is such a magical ice-cream van,' said Dad scornfully, 'ask her if she'd fix her windscreen wipers. It's starting to rain and I can't see a thing.'

With an extremely loud squeak, the windscreen wipers started up.

'Good grief,' said Dad, astounded.

'See!' cried Wendy and Wayne.

'I've just remembered,' exclaimed Mum. 'I did come across an old packet of sherbet, but I binned it.'

'It might still be in the bin,' said Wayne. 'That's if Gina hasn't sniffed it out and eaten it.'

'Baa!' said Gina from the back of the van,

where she was munching a bar of chocolate, wrapper and all.

'I'm not entirely sure I want to be responsible for people zapping and popping,' said Dad, as everyone rummaged for the Fizzbomb Sherbet in the rubbish Mum had emptied out of the bin on to the back lawn.

'But, Dad, it's a sensation. You said so yourself.'

'And it hasn't done us any harm.'

'That's true,' said Mum. 'And you two had guzzled plenty by the time I caught you last night.'

'NO, GINA!' everyone yelled as the goat waded into the rubbish pile and started chomping.

Dad marched her down the garden and tied her to the fence.

'No sign of it,' sighed Mum after they had searched and searched the rubbish pile. 'But what about trying some ordinary sherbet?' she suggested. 'Wouldn't that work?'

'Fizzbomb Sherbet is quite out-of-the-ordinary, Mum,' Wendy assured her.

'Hum-hmm-hum. Then we'll just have to see what we can do,' said Mum. 'Hum-hmm.'

She disappeared into the kitchen with a vague look on her face.

'She's humming. That means she's got one of her ideas coming on,' Wendy warned.

'I know,' said Dad. 'Keep clear.'

In bed that night, Wayne and Wendy found it hard to sleep through the strange smells and sounds coming from the kitchen.

'What's she doing?' said Wayne crossly. He pulled his pillow round his ears and the quilt up over his nose.

'Trying to invent fizzbombs. There's a whole lot of stuff out on the kitchen table.

Sherbet, baking soda, popcorn and bubble-gum. Anything that pops, fizzles or bubbles – Mum's trying it.'

'Won't work,' said Wayne from under his muffle of pillow and quilt.

BOOF! Something exploded softly in the kitchen.

'Yeek!' shrieked Mum.

Wendy and Wayne ran to the top of the stairs and watched a thick white cloud billow out from the kitchen and drift up the stairs. Downstairs, Mum coughed and choked while Dad spoke soothingly, in between splutters.

Wayne and Wendy giggled.

'Don't hear any fizzbombs,' said Wendy.

Wayne sighed. 'I really thought Potts of Ice-cream was going to work. I guess they'll give up now just like they always do.'

Both Wendy and Wayne had been hoping that Potts of Ice-cream would be the one idea that lasted, because then there would always be pots of ice-cream to guzzle, as much as any boy or girl could wish for.

At breakfast next morning, Mum was still cleaning up the debris from her fizzbomb experiments. She smiled wearily at the two children as she scooped marmalade ice-cream on to their toast.

'Never mind, Mum,' said Wayne. 'We'll have another search today for that other packet of sherbet. We might still find it.'

Baa-pip went something under the table.

Baa-pip-pip-pop!

'Oh, no,' groaned Wendy. 'It's Gina.'

Before anyone could move, the goat's frightened baas were drowned out by such an outburst of fizzbomb explosions it sounded as if a small volcano was erupting at their feet. The kitchen table rocked and jerked so much that everyone had to grab their breakfast to stop it hurtling across the room.

'Looks like Gina found the sherbet after all,' said Wayne, as Dad hauled the twitching goat out into the back garden.

'You know, Dad's ice-creams are so delicious that people will want to buy them, fizzbombs or not,' said Wendy. 'I'm sure they will.'

'Well, there's still a freezer full of ice-cream to sell,' said Mum, as she filled up a dish of water for Gina to drink. 'Maybe we should try.'

Wendy winked at Wayne as Dad came back in.

'Marshmallow Squidge is delumptious even without the fizzbombs,' she said loudly.

'And Chocwobble is totally slurpful,' nodded Wayne.

'I must admit I keep sneaking spoonfuls of Cheesy Peasmint myself,' Mum smiled.

'I'm surprised there's any ice-cream left to sell with all you guzzlers around,' said Dad.

'Hmm,' said Mum. She thought for a moment then tapped the table with a teaspoon. 'You are right, little Potts. Potts of Ice-cream is too good to give up on. It should be business as usual tonight. What do you say, Sam?'

Wendy and Wayne cheered.

'I don't think I have much choice,' grinned Dad. 'It's three against one.'

'Four,' reminded Wayne. 'Don't forget Macaroni.'

'That's right,' said Wendy. 'Macaroni wouldn't want us to give up. She'll make sure Potts of Ice-cream is a success. After all, she *is* a magical ice-cream van!'

3 **Macaroni on the loose**

'We can't shut up shop yet, Macaroni, there's a big queue outside,' exclaimed Dad, as the till drawer pinged shut, just missing his fingers.

Macaroni grumbled her engine impatiently.

'I think she's had enough,' said Mum. 'There's no point in arguing with her once she's made up her mind.'

'Sounds just like someone else we know, eh?' Dad winked at Wendy and Wayne.

Macaroni tooted her horn impatiently and revved her engine so hard that Dad dropped a scoopful of Stingy Strawberry on Gina's tail. The goat opened a dozy eye, twitched her tail, then gulped down the ice-cream before anyone could stop her.

'Watch out,' yelled Wayne, but it was too late.

As the ice-cream's hot chilli pepper hit Gina's tastebuds, her eyes watered and she began to baa and buck wildly with fright.

Everyone took cover in the driving cabin as sweets scattered and ice-cream splattered. Macaroni blared her horn in protest. The van rocked violently from side to side.

'Gina and Macaroni,' shouted Mum, 'behave yourselves!'

Wayne sat on Gina while Wendy prised her teeth apart and hastily stuffed in a coneful of Carrot and Coconut Cooldown. With Gina calmed, Macaroni quietened and pinged open her peacock till.

'Thank you,' said Dad. 'Except it's too late. The queue's been scared off by the rumpus. Home, gang.'

It was the dead of night and all was still. Wendy opened her eyes, suddenly awake. A strange noise echoed in her head but when she strained to listen all she could hear was the sleepy rumble of snoring from Mum and Dad's room.

'I must have been dreaming,' thought Wendy, and she snuggled back under her quilt.

PING-TRRRING!

Wendy sat bolt upright.

PING-TRRRING! PING-TRRRING! PING-TRRRRIIIIING!

She rubbed the sleep from her eyes. She wasn't dreaming now.

Wendy climbed from her top bunk and shook her brother hard. It generally took a lot of hard shaking to waken Wayne.

'Umph,' grunted Wayne from under his quilt.

PING-TRRRING! went the strange noise.

Wendy opened the window. The ice-cream van was parked in the driveway.

PING-TRRRING!

Now she was properly awake, Wendy recognised the noise. It was Macaroni pinging her till open and shut.

'Macaroni – what's wrong?' she hissed. 'Shush. You'll waken the whole street.'

Everything was still again, then Macaroni flashed each of her fairy lights, one by one, faster and faster.

'Whatsheupto?' yawned Wayne, kneeling up to look out of the window.

'Don't know,' said Wendy slowly. 'But Gina's sleeping in Macaroni again tonight. Maybe she's up to something.'

JANGLE! sang out Macaroni. TOOT! BRRRM! revved her engine.

'Oh, help,' said Wendy. 'She wouldn't –'

'She *is*,' groaned Wayne.

The children ran out of the house in their pyjamas, just as Macaroni sped off down the street. They called after her as loudly as they dared and she braked to a halt, then reversed swiftly and ended up on the front lawn.

'I don't believe it. Look who's driving!' gasped Wayne.

Gina the goat sat in the driver's seat, her front hooves perched on the steering wheel.

'Let's get her out.'

But Gina wouldn't budge. Wayne climbed in the front to soothe the goat while Wendy got some chocolate from the back of the van to entice her out.

Neither of the children noticed the sly rumble of Macaroni's engine until it was too late.

'Oh no, she's off again,' cried Wendy. 'Macaroni, stop!'

'Seatbelts on,' said Wayne, as the van gathered speed. 'You too, Gina.'

Macaroni sped out of their street and on to the main road.

JANGLE! she sang out excitedly, as she wheeled off into the night.

The dark, empty road seemed endless. But at long last Macaroni trundled to a stop. Wendy and Wayne climbed out.

'Where on earth are we?' asked Wendy.

A cool, salty wind billowed their pyjamas. The skreek of a gull sounded in the dark and, in front of them, a long stretch of silver rolled and folded with a soothing thunder.

Macaroni jangled quietly and flickered all her lights.

'We're at the seaside!' cried Wayne.

'Come on, Gina, time you got some exercise,' called Wendy, as she and Wayne raced off across sandy hillocks down to the sea which glimmered and shimmered with moonbeams.

The two children and the goat chased each other in and out of the waves until the dark lightened to grey and a gleam of fiery sun appeared on the horizon.

'Sunrise,' said Wayne sadly. 'We'll have to go soon.'

'I'm starving,' said Wendy. 'Ooh, I think I'll have a packet of crisps, some lemonade, a bar of chocolate . . .'

'Poor old Macaroni,' said Wayne, as they made their way back to the van. 'I bet she wishes she could have been splashing about with us.'

'Don't give her any ideas,' said Wendy. 'Oh, but she does look lonely. Hey, Macaroni, we're back.'

But as they sat in the ice-cream van's cabin, munching a pile of goodies and watching the sun rise high over the sea, the two children heard Macaroni make the oddest noise.

'I hope she's not broken down,' said Wayne.

'Do you think she's got sand in her engine?' Wendy wondered.

Puzzled, they got out, opened the bonnet and listened to the noise. It was a kind of trembly, hiccupy jangle that ended in a forlorn toot.

Wayne frowned. 'You know, if an ice-cream van could cry, I think it would sound something like that.'

'Wayne,' said Wendy, 'remember when Mum cleaned her out? She said Macaroni must have been a seaside ice-cream van. She had sand and seashells inside.'

'And there was the burst beach-ball in her horn,' remembered Wayne.

'This must be her old home. She's homesick for the seaside,' said Wendy. 'What'll we do?'

Macaroni gave a great tremble.

'There, there,' said Wayne, and he patted her bonnet a little awkwardly. After all, how *did* you make a homesick ice-cream van feel better?

Gina looked up at Macaroni with soft, butter-fudge eyes and rubbed against her bumper.

'You know,' said Wendy, 'everyone's always telling those two what a naughty, badly behaved pair of pests they are. But we do love them. You can cuddle a goat but maybe Macaroni is feeling bad because she thinks we don't love her.'

'Well, that's silly,' said Wayne. He scuffed up some sand with his toe.

'*We* know that, but what if *she* doesn't?' argued Wendy. 'Gina too,' she added, removing a string of seaweed from the goat's head. 'Maybe that's why they were running away from home.'

Wayne scuffed some more with his toes until he had made quite a sand cloud.

'Baa-wheesh,' Gina sneezed.

'Stop that, Wayne,' said Wendy. 'Just say it. Go on.'

'You say it,' said Wayne.

'Oh, honestly,' said Wendy. 'Macaroni and Gina, you're a couple of crazy crackers but we love you. We really do.'

She stared hard at her brother.

Wayne coughed. 'I bet there isn't another ice-cream van or a goat quite like you two in the whole world,' he declared. 'And that's the truth.'

He ruffled Gina's ears and, with his pyjama leg, he polished a crust of salt spray from Macaroni's bumper until it gleamed with the sunbeams that now spilled all across the sea.

Macaroni stopped hiccuping. She sat quiet for a moment then, without warning, burst into a verse of 'Yankee Doodle Dandy'.

'She's feeling better,' said Wayne.

Wendy nodded. 'I wish we could stay here longer. It's going to be a beautiful day. But Mum and Dad will go bananas if they wake up and find us missing.'

'We'll come back another time,' promised Wayne. 'A hard-working ice-cream van deserves a day off.'

Macaroni was silent. Wayne and Wendy looked at each other. What on earth were they going to do if she refused to budge? Here they were, stuck at the seaside, far from home, wearing only their pyjamas.

There was a faint rumble from Macaroni's engine. She let out a loud cough and revved up. She was ready for home, after all.

'Where did all this sand come from?' shrieked Mum. She was stocking up sweets and crisps in the back of the van. 'It's everywhere!'

With a mystified look on his face, Dad pulled a slimy strand of seaweed off the steering wheel.

Wendy and Wayne stifled yawns and tried to look wide-awake and innocent.

'That goat must be dragging sand in with her,' said Mum. 'Though where she got it from I don't know.'

'Beach-balls, fizzbombs, seaweed — what next?' muttered Dad.

'But you two are always saying you don't want life to be ordinary and boring,' said Wendy. 'It's never boring with Macaroni and Gina around.'

'And if it wasn't for them, Potts of Ice-cream would never have been such a hit,' Wayne pointed out.

'That's true,' said Mum sheepishly. 'We've never exactly been a rip-roaring success before.'

'But we are now,' admitted Dad. 'Macaroni and Gina, we're sorry. We couldn't have done all this without you.'

'They deserve a reward,' said Wendy. 'It's only fair.'

'I know just the thing,' exclaimed Wayne, as if he'd only just thought of it. 'Let's all have a day out at the seaside!'

4 **Macaroni to the rescue**

'All right, Macaroni,' said Dad at the end of the Sunday evening ice-cream run. 'You've worked hard today so you deserve a run. Not too far though. It's getting late.'

Macaroni revved her engine excitedly and took off on one of her favourite detours past the railway bridge, where she wouldn't budge until she had flashed and tooted at the eight o'clock train.

Now the wilful ice-cream van veered left instead of turning right into the road that would take them home.

'Macaroni, this is very bad behaviour,' said Wayne, as sternly as he could. Secretly, he was delighted by the antics of the ice-cream van, for the longer Macaroni kept misbehaving, the further away was Wayne and Wendy's bedtime.

They ended up at the carnival.

'No,' said Mum firmly, as Wendy and Wayne gazed longingly at the whirling, glittering lights of the big wheel.

'I'm afraid not. You two have school in the morning. Home, Macaroni.'

It was Mum's no-arguing voice. Macaroni spluttered and rumbled her engine in protest, but in the end she took them out of the carnival field and on to the road home.

'It's a bit cold for swimming,' said Wendy, as they passed some bathers in the boating pond. 'No, hang on. Macaroni, stop!'

The ice-cream van screeched to a halt.

Everyone peered through the trees at the boating pond.

Two heads bobbed in the middle of the water.

'Help!' shouted a man's voice. It came from one of the bobbing heads. From the other came the sound of frantic barking.

'They're in trouble,' said Dad. 'We'll get you out,' he yelled, running for the lifebuoy on the other side of the pond.

'Keep swimming,' called Mum, and she raced to untie one of the rowing boats at the side of the pond.

'I'll find a branch or a stick,' said Wendy.

'One of them's swimming to the side,' cried Wayne. 'Look, it's the dog. But the man keeps slipping under the water.'

Dad had unfastened the lifebuoy and

Mum had the rowing boat ready, but before either of them could do any more Macaroni began revving her engine to such a pitch that Gina the goat scampered out of the back door in fright.

Blaring her horn and flashing all her lights, Macaroni crashed into the water and surged forward until she reached the struggling man. Then she cut dead her engine and stayed perfectly still and quiet, even though she was filling up with water and sinking fast. The man clambered on to her bonnet, then up on to her roof, which stayed clear above the water.

Mum and Dad rowed over to Macaroni and helped the man off the van's roof and into the boat.

'I went in to rescue the dog,' shivered the man, as he climbed from the boat. 'He was tangled in pond weed, but once I freed him I found I was tangled in it myself. I can't thank you and, er, your van, enough.'

Puzzled, he looked over at Macaroni, sunk deep in the pond. The dog shook a spray of water from his coat then barked and wagged his tail gratefully at the ice-cream van.

Some time later, a recovery truck dragged Macaroni out of the water. Pond scum clung to her paintwork and when they wrenched open her doors a flood of weeds and pond creatures splashed on to the ground.

'That was a very brave thing to do, Macaroni,' said Mum.

The ice-cream van gave a watery gurgle from her loudspeaker horn, which dislodged a frog or two. One headlamp flickered then died. Her engine gave a feeble cough, then Macaroni was still.

'She's very sick, isn't she?' said Wayne.

'I'll give you a warm soapy scrub as soon as we're home,' said Wendy.

'I think it'll take more than that, little Pott,' said Mum gently.

'She'll need a complete overhaul,' said the recovery man. 'And even then ...'

'She was hardly in the best shape to start with,' said Dad. 'Poor old girl.'

Next day, the Potts family arrived at the garage. Wendy and Wayne led Gina on a piece of string.

'There she is!' said Mum. 'She looks much better today.'

But she wasn't. Macaroni was dried out, clean and polished, but she couldn't be started.

'She needs a whole new engine,' said the mechanic, shaking his head.

'She deserves a rest,' said Dad.

Mum nodded sadly as Macaroni was once again loaded on to the recovery truck.

'I think I know just the place,' she said at last. 'The farm that took our goats has such beautiful views over the countryside. I can't think of a nicer place to retire to. I wonder if I could persuade the farmer that Macaroni would make an excellent little goat shelter.'

'But she might want to go back to the seaside,' said Wayne.

'That's her favourite place,' said Wendy.

'Would she be safe there?' Mum worried. 'And it's much further away. We wouldn't be able to visit her so often. She might be lonely.'

'We should let Macaroni decide,' said Wayne.

'That's right,' Wendy agreed. 'Macaroni,

you're too sick and tired to work any more. Where would you like to be – the farm with all the goats to keep you company, or the seaside?'

'A jangle for the farm and a toot for the seaside,' suggested Wayne.

Macaroni was still.

'Maybe she's lost her voice,' sighed Wendy. 'She was in that cold pond for a long time.'

A small, croaky sound came from Macaroni's loudspeaker horn. Then she tried a gentle jingle. Finally, she let out a wobbly but very definite JANGLE!

'The farm!' yelled Wendy and Wayne.

At the farm, Macaroni was lowered on to the grass. Wendy and Wayne climbed in the back of the van to say goodbye. Macaroni still smelled damply of pond water, and it seemed strange to see her shelves bare again. But the mottled mirror tiles still cast a magical, rainbow glimmer.

'You'll make a very special little shelter,' said Wendy. 'And you won't be lonely with all those goats.'

'Bye, Macaroni,' said Wayne. 'We'll come back and visit very soon.'

The ice-cream van gave a contented toot then sat quietly jingling as the goats gambolled and grazed in the field around her.

Mum came back, walking sideways in an effort to hide the box she carried under her arm.

'What a nice farmer,' she said. 'I convinced him that goats love Macaroni and told him we'd come back every week to clean her out.'

'We've lost Gina,' Wayne noticed, as they walked back down the hillside.

There was a loud BAA-AA behind them. At the top of the hill Gina kicked up her back legs and frolicked off into the field with the rest of the goats.

'I didn't think that animal had an atom of energy in her,' said Dad. 'Look at her go!'

'There wasn't really room for her to gambol about in our house,' said Wendy. 'Now she can be a proper goat again.'

'They'll look after each other,' said Mum, sniffing a little. Then she coughed loudly, in an effort to disguise the noises that were coming from the box under her arm.

Wendy and Wayne looked at each other and groaned as they heard the cluck-clucking and flip-flap-flutterings.

'There's a hen in that box,' said Dad. 'Don't pretend there isn't.'

'Three actually,' admitted Mum. 'I was reading just the other day that hens fed on the finest herbs can produce the most delicious eggs you've ever tasted. There's a market for that sort of thing these days.' She smiled dreamily. 'They'll spend their days in the garden listening to music. I'll read them poetry. They'll be the happiest of hens and lay the best-tasting eggs ever. Hum-hmm-hum.'

'Wouldn't mind being a hen myself,' muttered Dad, as Mum hummed tunelessly.

'I think it's an EGGSellent idea,' laughed Wendy. 'Though hens will be a bit boring after Macaroni and Gina.'

'EGGSeedingly,' chuckled Wayne. 'But with Mum and Dad in charge something's bound to go wrong.'

Mum and Dad exchanged glances.

'We must be the most EGGSasperating parents,' said Dad.

'EGGStremely annoying,' agreed Mum.

'Yes, but we're used to you,' grinned Wendy.

'And now we can have eggs instead of ice-cream on toast for breakfast,' said Wayne happily. 'I never ever thought I'd get sick of eating ice-cream – but I am!'